This igloo book belongs to:

....

igloobooks

Original story by Anna Sewell
Retold by Melanie Joyce
Illustrated by Diane Le Feyer

Designed by Justine Ablett
Edited by Stephanie Moss

An imprint of Igloo Books Group,
a Bonnier Publishing company
www.bonnierpublishing.com

Published in 2018
by Igloo Books Ltd, Cottage Farm
Sywell, NN6 0BJ

Manufactured in China. GUA006 0818
10 9 8 7 6 5 4 3 2 1

Library of Congress Cataloging-in-Publication
Data is available upon request.

ISBN 978-1-4998-8151-6
IglooBooks.com
www.bonnierpublishing.com

Black Beauty

igloobooks

My early home, and the first place I can remember well, was a large, pleasant meadow with trees and a pond of clear water in it. I lived with my mother, who was named Duchess. In the daytime I ran by her side, and at night I lay down close to her.

There were some young horses that lived in the meadow, too, but my mother said they were cart horses. **"You are well bred,"** she said. **"I want you to grow to be gentle and not kick or bite."** I never forgot my mother's advice, for she was a wise old horse.

Time passed in that happy place, and I grew to be handsome. My coat was soft and glossy black. I had one white foot and a pretty white star on my forehead. Then, when I was four years old, my master said I was to be broken in.

Breaking in meant that I had to
learn to wear a saddle and bridle. . .

. . . and to carry a man,
woman, or child on my back.

I was to be taught to have a carriage fixed behind me and always
to obey my master's will, without the freedom of my early life.

My training was soon complete, and early that May I was bought by a Squire Gordon and taken to Birtwick Park. At the stables, I was put in a comfortable stall that was clean and airy. Next to me was a fat gray pony named Merrylegs, who thought himself very handsome indeed.

Across the way was a chestnut mare, looking over from her stall.
Like me, she was about fifteen hands high, but she seemed bad-tempered.
"That's Ginger," said Merrylegs. **"People have been unkind to her, so she snaps and bites sometimes, even though our grooms, John and James, are very kind."**

I soon settled into my new home. Squire Gordon was a good rider, and named me Black Beauty because my coat was dark and shiny.

As time went on, I was put in the carriage with Ginger. She told me about her early life and how she had been cruelly treated.

I knew it was gentleness that Ginger needed, for I had heard a man
say that a bad-tempered master never made a good-tempered horse.
With time, Ginger grew much less cross. She and Merrylegs became
my dearest friends, and we had many adventures at Birtwick Park.

One stormy night, I was pulling a cart over a flooding river and felt something was wrong. **"Go on, Beauty,"** said my master, but I would not.

"Stop!" shouted a man suddenly.
"The bridge is broken!"
Master said I had saved him and that
animals knew things that their owners did not.

Another time, our master went to town for business, and I was stabled there for the night with Ginger. As John settled us down, I noticed a man with a pipe come in.

I thought nothing of it until later, when I saw a red light and a thick, gray cloud across the stalls.

Someone shouted, **"Fire!"** But John spoke gently to me and led me outside.

I whinnied because I could not see Ginger, but at last James brought her out, too. She said that if I had not called to her, she would not have had the courage to move.

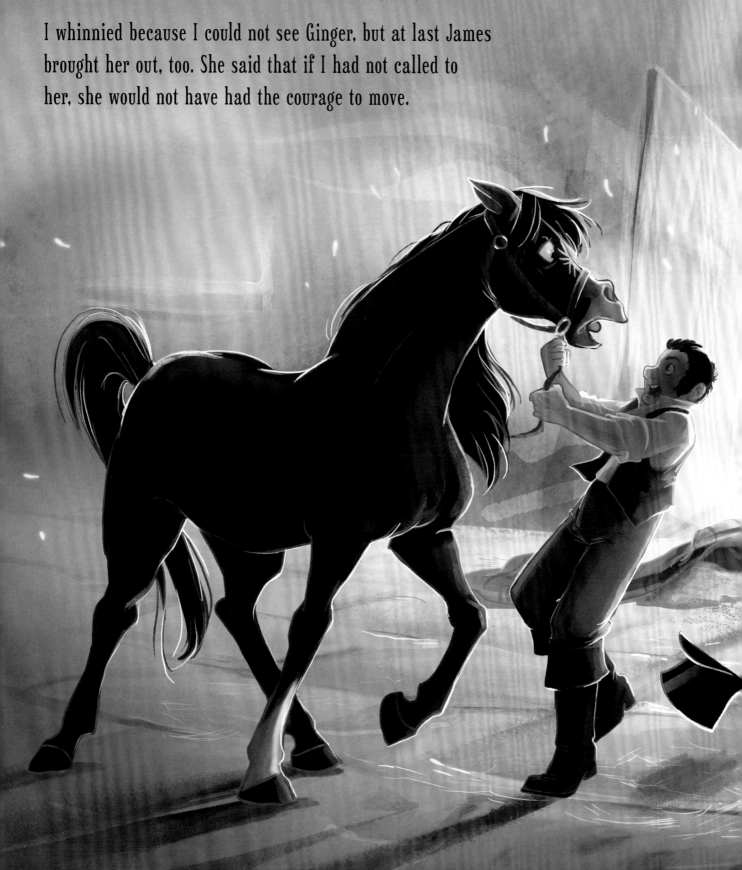

Soon after that terrible night, James left and a new groom, Joe Green, arrived. He was kind, but inexperienced.

One night, the mistress fell ill and I raced to the doctor's house. I was hot from galloping, so Joe did not put my rug on and I caught a terrible chill.

John looked after me and I soon became well again, but it was not the same for my mistress. Her health was poor, and we soon learned that she and the master were to move to a warmer climate.

I was sold with Ginger to an Earl, and Merrylegs was given to a vicar.

After three happy years at Birtwick Hall, we said a sad goodbye to our old friend Merrylegs, as Joe and John rode us to our new home at Earlshall Park. I held my face close to John's when he left, as that was all I could do to say goodbye.

Earlshall was bigger than Birtwick Park, but not as pleasant. The lady of the house insisted that Ginger and I wear the bearing rein, which kept our heads high and was uncomfortable.

Ginger kicked out in annoyance and never pulled the carriage again.

As for me, worse was to come.

I was cared for by a groom named Reuben Smith. He was a good man, but he was careless, and this was his downfall. One night when the master was away, he rode me home from town. There were sharp stones on the road and I lost a shoe, but he forced me to gallop.

I went at such a speed, I stumbled and fell on my knees. I quickly got up, but Reuben had fallen off and was lying on the ground. He groaned, then lay still. He was dead.

Everyone knew I was not to blame, but my knees were damaged and I needed a long rest.

I was put into a paddock by myself and felt
very lonely, until one day, Ginger arrived.
I was so happy to see her and to have that
time together.

But it was not long after that
I was taken away and sold,
with only a sad whinny of
goodbye to my dear old friend.

In my time after Earlshall, I became a job horse and was rented out to anyone that wished to hire me. There were many bad drivers, but some good ones, too. Because I was patient and good-natured, one such driver recommended me to a man named Mr. Barry, who became my new owner.

My master knew little about horses, but he treated me well.
I would have had an easy time of it, had it not been for one
groom who stole my feeding oats to sell, and another, Alfred
Smirk, who did not clean my stable properly.

My feet became so tender
and sore that I fell lame.

Mr. Barry discovered the truth, and made sure I was fed and cared for.
But he was so annoyed at being deceived by the two grooms, he decided
not to keep a horse any longer. When my feet were better, I was sold
again, this time to a horse-cab driver named Jeremiah Barker.

Jerry, as Jeremiah was known, was a good master, and I had never known such a happy family. Jerry's wife Polly, his daughter Dolly, and his son Harry petted and fussed over me. I was stabled with their old white horse, Captain, and we were well looked after.

What a team Jerry and I made, trotting past traffic, through the streets of London. The days were long, but I was happy in my work. Then, one winter, after nights spent waiting in the cold, Jerry fell ill. He was no longer able to work and, sadly, sent me to be sold.

My life as a cab horse after that was very hard indeed. I was so overworked that I became exhausted and ended up at a horse fair. Thin and worn out, I had all but lost hope when I was bought by a kind man named Farmer Thoroughgood.

Even though I was in a poor condition, Farmer Thoroughgood knew I was well bred. He said that I had seen better days, but with rest and care, I would soon recover. This was true, for after a winter of good food and a comfortable stable, I was like my old self again.

When the summer came, Farmer Thoroughgood
said he had found the perfect home for me.
I was carefully groomed until my coat shone.

My mane was combed and
my hooves were painted.

Then, I was taken to a pretty house about a
mile down the road, where three ladies lived.

Miss Blomefield, Miss Ellen, and Miss Lavinia were my new owners, and liked me very much. A groom came to feed me and noticed the white star on my forehead and my one white foot.

"Why, it's Black Beauty!"
he cried, for it was Joe Green.

Joe was the best and kindest of grooms, and the ladies promised I would never be sold. I had nothing to fear and, at last, all my troubles were over.

Sometimes, however, I would wake at night and imagine I was still in the orchard at Birtwick Park, standing with my old friends under the apple tree.

Discover all eight enchanting classic tales...

Alice in Wonderland

Join Alice and tumble down the rabbit hole into Wonderland, where nothing is as it seems. This beautiful book is perfect for creating the most magical of story times for every little reader.

Black Beauty

Rediscover this moving story of one horse's trials and hardships in this classic tale. When Black Beauty grows to be a handsome stallion, he is passed from one owner to the next, but will he ever be free?

The Jungle Book

Join Mowgli as he learns the strange ways of the jungle, guided wisely by Baloo the bear. This retelling of the timeless classic, with beautiful illustrations, will capture every child's imagination.

Oliver Twist

Dive into the life of pickpocketing crooks in this captivating tale. Follow poor little orphan Oliver all the way from the workhouse until he meets Fagin's gang. Can he escape the streets?

The Secret Garden

Unlock the door to a magical place, full of beauty and mystery. Mary Lennox is lonely and spoiled, but when she discovers a garden hidden in the grounds, it will change her family forever.

Treasure Island

Set sail on a rip-roaring adventure in this classic tale of swashbuckling pirates and hidden treasure. This exciting tale, with stunning original illustrations, is perfect for a thrilling story time.

The Wind in the Willows

Join Mole and his friends for a riverbank adventure in this classic tale of friendship. Can Mole, Ratty, and Badger keep the mischievous Mr. Toad out of trouble? Find out in this beautiful, timeless classic.

The Wizard of Oz

Be swept away with Dorothy and Toto to the Land of Oz, where they meet Scarecrow, Tin Man, and Lion. This retelling of the well-loved classic story is sure to make story time exciting.

igloobooks